THE
FINTASTIC
FISHSITTER

To the original Sami and all the other amazing kids in my life, especially Daniel and Charlotte.

—M. O.

To my wife Hannah and son Oscar. Love you loads!

—M. J.

A FEIWEL AND FRIENDS BOOK
An Imprint of Macmillan

 Printed in China by RR Donnelley Asia Printing Solutions Ltd., Dongguan City, Guangdong Province. For information, address Feiwel and Friends, 175 Fifth Avenue, New York, N.Y. 10010.

Feiwel and Friends books may be purchased for business or promotional use. For information on bulk purchases, please contact the Macmillan Corporate and Premium Sales Department at (800) 221-7945 x5442 or by e-mail at specialmarkets@macmillan.com.

Library of Congress Cataloging-in-Publication Data Available

ISBN: 978-1-250-06523-0

Book design by Anna Booth

Feiwel and Friends logo designed by Filomena Tuosto

First Edition: 2016

10 9 8 7 6 5 4 3 2 1

mackids.com

MO O'HARA

MAREK JAGUCKI

FEIWEL AND FRIENDS
NEW YORK

I'm Tom and this is my best friend Pradeep, who lives next door.

We have a big fat zombie goldfish named Frankie.

Unfortunately, my big brother Mark has a cute but evil vampire kitten named Fang.

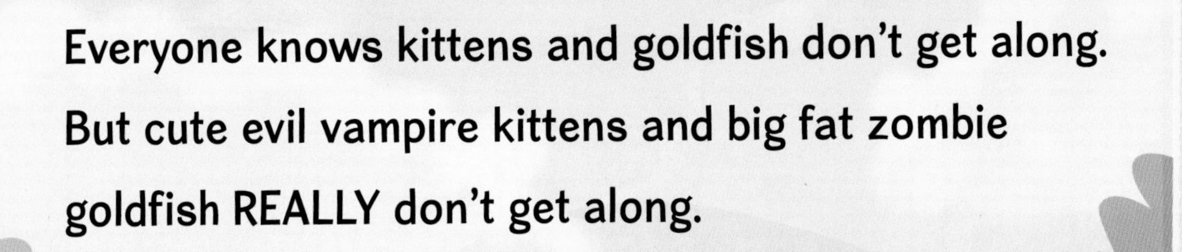

Everyone knows kittens and goldfish don't get along. But cute evil vampire kittens and big fat zombie goldfish REALLY don't get along.

So when we asked Pradeep's little sister Sami to look after Frankie, we thought we should give her some helpful tips . . .

SIX REALLY IMPORTANT TIPS FOR ~~BABYSITTING~~ FISH-SITTING A ZOMBIE GOLDFISH:

1. Keep Fang away from Frankie

2. Zombie goldfish only eat green food (moldy Brussels sprouts, green jelly beans, stinky pond slime)

3. All kittens can be pretty sneaky, but Fang is SUPER sneaky

4. Watch out for Frankie's eyes—he can hypnotize you

5. Did we mention that Fang the vampire kitten is TROUBLE?

6. Seriously, keep Fang away from Frankie!

I think we made our point.

Sami showed right away that
she would be a great fish-sitter . . .

when she eventually figured out what she was supposed to do.

She took her fish-sitting responsibilities very seriously.

Sami drew a plan for a Fishy Protection Zone
with booby traps to keep out cute evil vampire kittens.

She even added a lookout tower and took turns with Frankie to keep watch.

But kittens are sneaky—and Fang is SUPER sneaky, with extra-sneaky sprinkles on top.

She is also a master
of disguise.

In no time, Fang had
managed to sneak up
behind Sami and
Frankie and . . .

POUNCE!

Fur flew and fins flailed!

Teeth snapped and tails thwacked!

Claws were bared and green eyes stared!

"Naughty kitty!" Sami shouted.

She put her hands on her hips
and used her best cross mom voice.
"Put Frankie down right this instant!"

Just as Sami was about to order Fang to leave,
Fang turned on her special power of kitty cuteness.

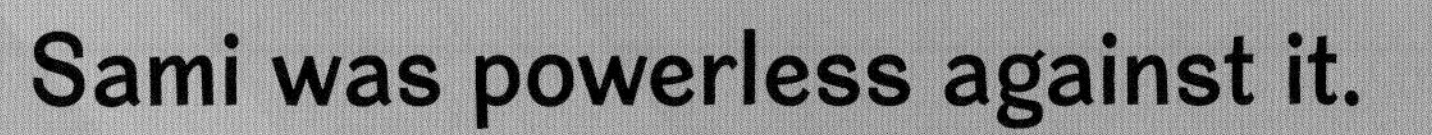

Sami was powerless against it.

"I suppose we could all play together," she said.

"I could kitty-sit too!"

Fang and Frankie imagined the fun games they each wanted to play.

Unfortunately, Fang and Frankie found it difficult to play nicely together.

They couldn't agree on a game that didn't end up with somebody being

swooshed,

squashed,

splashed . . .

or ZOMBIFIED.

"If you can't play your games nicely," said Sami, "then we'll play MY game instead!"

But Sami's game was
NOT their idea of fun.

When Pradeep and I got home, we couldn't believe Fang and Frankie were playing together! And they were being . . . nice.

We told Sami she was the most fintastic fish-sitter ever! She totally deserved the extra scoops of ice cream we gave her to say thanks.

Maybe cute evil vampire kittens and big fat zombie goldfish CAN get along after all. . . .

Well,
sometimes.